Mommy and Daddy took me to explore new homes. _____ came with us. _____ was our Realtor®. Some of the yards were jungles. One of the jungles had a tire swing. Another one had a sandbox.

There were a lot of rooms to explore inside. I found a lot of new places to hide.

We went to one that had gray walls. Mommy and Daddy really liked this one. _____ let me pick a bedroom at this one!

When we went home Mommy and Daddy asked me which home I wanted to live in. I told them "the gray home".

I asked if my friend Cora could still live next door. Mommy told me "No", and I was sad, but Mommy said I would make new friends and that Cora could come play too! That made me happy!

We went to a new park to play and I made a new friend. His name is Warren. He lives close to the gray home!

Then we took a walk. Mommy and Daddy said we were going to the gray home, but we stopped in front of a yellow home.

I asked Mommy and Daddy when we were going to the gray home. They said we were here. "But it's Yellow!" I said. They reminded me that the inside is gray.

"It's the gray home that's yellow!" I said. Mommy and Daddy laughed with me.

We went home and I helped pack all of my toys into boxes, and we stacked the boxes in the living room. I like to pretend the boxes are a city!

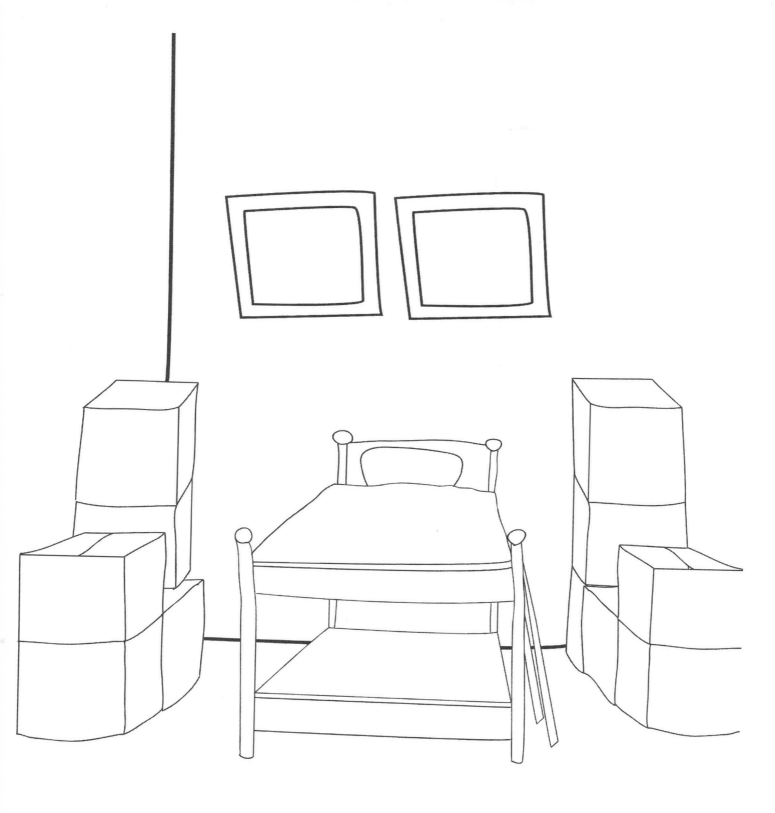

Daddy brought me home a big boy bed. He told me it's for my new gray home. My new bed made a great tower for my city.

I asked Mommy and Daddy when I can play at the gray home. They told me soon! I asked if I could bring my city. I was very excited when they told me yes!

Today I went to play with Auntie Joanna and Uncle John. We saw a movie. Then we went to play on the slide.

I missed my Mommy, so Auntie Joann called her. "Where are you?" I asked Mommy. "I'm at the gray home setting up your city," she said. "Can I come to the gray home?" I asked. Mommy said yes.

When I got to the gray home, my big city was all set up inside! I took Aunt Joann to see my new bedroom. It was different, and perfect! My dresser was there. My book shelf was there. All my toys were there. And... my big boy bed was there!!!!

I climbed up the stairs and sat at the top. It was very high. Then I heard knocking. I ran to the door with Mommy.

My new friend _____ was there with pizza. This is the best day ever! I asked _____ to come see my new room. When we got to my room I said, "My name is Aiden. I have a big boy bed and this is My New Gray Home!"

When it was time for bed, Daddy climbed to the top of my tall bed and read me a story. When the story was over and it was time to go to sleep I wasn't scared to be in my new room because I knew the grey home is where I belong.

THE END

What does your new home look like?

Draw your new home here!

What do you look forward to in your new home?

Draw something you are excited about at your new home on the next 3 pages.

Draw your bedroom at your new home.